Best Mates Too!

Best Mates Too!

By Bob Hartman

Illustrated by
Mark Beech

15 14 13 12 11 10   8 7 6 5 4 3 2 1

First published 2010 by Authentic Media Ltd
Milton Keynes
www.authenticmedia.co.uk

British Library Cataloguing in Publication Data
A catalogue record for this book is available from the British Library

ISBN: 978-1-86024-805-4

Cover and illustrations by Mark Beech
Page layout by Temple design
Creative direction by Pupfish
Printed in Great Britain by Bell & Bain Ltd, Glasgow

This book has been produced using paper from a sustainable source.

For Jeremiah

Contents

Chapter 1
Tax

Jesus jumped out of the boat and waded to shore. And so did his disciples, with Pip, Tommo, and Big Bart bringing up the rear.

'It's good to be back,' grinned Pip. 'Back in Capernaum-by-the Sea!'

'But what a trip!' sighed Bart. 'There was that big storm, for a start.'

'And that crazy naked demon guy.

And that angry mob. And those suicidal pigs!' added Tommo.

'Where did Jesus say we were going next?' asked Bart.

'To see the tax collector,' answered Pip.

'He didn't happen to say WHICH tax collector, did he?' asked Tommo.

'No, why?' said Pip.

'No reason,' Tommo shrugged. 'Just curious.'

'I hate tax collectors,' said Bart.

'Me too,' Pip grunted. 'They're cheats, you know. They take lots more than they're supposed to, and just keep the extra for themselves.'

'And they're traitors,' added Tommo. 'They work for our Roman masters.'

Bart looked amazed. 'I did not know any of that,' he admitted.

'Then why do you hate them?' asked Pip.

'It's obvious, isn't it?' Bart shrugged. 'When you give them your money, they never give you anything back! At every other stall in the market-place, you give the man your money and you get a blanket or a coat or a juicy slice of goat-on-a-stick. But when the tax collector takes your money, you get nothing. Not even a thank-you.'

'What's obvious, Bart,' Tommo sighed, 'is that you have no idea what a tax collector does or how the tax system works.'

'Yeah, big guy,' Pip agreed, 'you don't get anything back because they use that money to build things – like roads and bridges.'

'And palaces. And fortresses,' Tommo added. 'And armies. To enslave and oppress our people. Like I said. Traitors.'

Bart scratched his head, 'So why don't we just stop giving them the money?'

And both Pip and Tommo sighed.

'Because they would kill us,' Tommo explained.

'I see,' Bart nodded. 'That's a fair trade. Now I understand how the tax system works!'

'And look,' said Pip. 'There's the tax collector. He's talking to Jesus.'

Bart waved. Pip sighed again. And Tommo disappeared.

'He's hiding behind me,' Bart whispered to Pip.

So Pip slipped quietly behind Bart as well and whispered, 'What's the problem, Tommo? You don't, by any chance, owe that man some money, do you?'

'Could do,' said Tommo. 'Might do. Probably do.'

'Well, you could pay it to him now,' Bart whispered. And then he added, 'Why are we whispering?'

'Because I do not have the money to pay him,' Tommo explained. 'And I do not want him to see me. Or the thugs standing behind him either.'

'Because they will kill you!' Bart exclaimed. 'I'm catching on, aren't I!'

'Shhhhh!' shushed Pip and Tommo.

'This is serious!' said Tommo. 'That tax collector's name is Matthew – and he is the worst! You know how people are always complaining that their taxes are costing them an arm and a leg? Well, you don't pay Matthew and he sends his goons around to break things. And an arm and a leg is usually where they start!'

Bart put a finger to his chin. 'So they don't kill you right away,' he concluded. 'Just a bit at a time. That's fair.'

'It's not fair!' Pip protested. 'It's all about forcing as much money out of you as they can. That Matthew has grown rich on other people's suffering. He ought to be ashamed.'

Just then, Jesus turned to face his friends.

'I have good news!' he announced. 'I have been talking with Matthew, here, and he has decided to join us. Say hello to my newest disciple!'

'I'm shocked,' said Pip.

'I'm puzzled,' said Bart.

'I'm doomed,' whimpered Tommo.

'What's more,' Jesus continued, 'he has invited all of us to his house tonight for a slap-up meal. He wants us to meet his friends. So get yourselves ready, dress up nice and proper, and I'll see you at Matthew's place for tea.'

The disciples wandered away in every direction, but Pip, Tommo and Big Bart wandered away the fastest! And when they were out of sight of the tax collector's booth, Tommo turned to the others and said, 'I'm not going! I can't go! That's all there is to it.'

'But Jesus asked us to go,' said Bart, 'so we have to. We're supposed to follow him wherever he leads us.'

'That's easy for you to say,' Tommo groaned. 'He's not leading you to a certain and painful death!'

'I think that's a little extreme, Tommo,' said Pip. 'I mean, if Matthew is following Jesus, too – if he's one of us now – then he's hardly going to break your legs.'

'But what about his friends?' Tommo argued. 'I owe him money. He owes them money. So maybe they decide to collect from me. Did you see the size of the goons that were with him? What if they've been invited too?'

Bart smiled. 'Goons. I like that word. Goons.'

'You're not helping,' Pip muttered.

'I beg to differ,' said Bart. 'I am helping. For I have already come up with a brilliant plan.'

Tommo shook his head. 'Brilliant. Plan. Bart. Three words that do not usually go together.'

But Bart would not be deterred. 'That's because you never met my Aunt Athalia. She was a master of disguise!'

'Do tell,' Pip sighed. 'Because you're going to do it anyway.'

'She was so good,' Bart explained, 'that none of us ever knew what she really looked like. A beautiful maiden, one day. A horrible hag the next. A cow. A goose. A cactus. She could make herself look like anything!'

'And she did this because . . . ?' Pip wondered.

'Because it was her hobby!' Bart grinned. 'Everyone needs a hobby. That's what her husband, Uncle Hedediah, used to say. His hobby was dirt.'

'What? Making things out of dirt?' asked Tommo. 'Searching for things in dirt?'

'No. Just dirt,' said Bart. 'He had an amazing collection. He was very protective of it. Kept most of it on his body.'

'So if we go to your Aunt Athalia,' said Pip. 'She'll make a disguise for Tommo?'

'Not likely,' said Bart. 'Aunt Athalia has been gone lo these many years. It's a sad story. She was disguised as a baby bunny. A cute and cuddly little thing. An amazing costume. She was crossing the road, just minding her own business, when an eagle swooped down from the sky, plucked her up in its powerful talons and carried her away.'

'That is a sad story,' Tommo agreed. 'So your aunt was eaten by an eagle.'

'I didn't say she was eaten!' Bart protested. 'I just said she was gone. She sent us a letter, many years later, explaining everything – how the eagle had carried her to its nest, and upon discovering its mistake, promptly kicked her out, from whence she stumbled unharmed into the nearest village.'

'So she never came back?' asked Pip.

'Her husband was covered with dirt,' Bart shrugged. 'Would you?'

'So how does any of this information help?' cried Tommo.

'Because,' Bart explained, 'Aunt Athalia passed on to me, her favourite nephew, many of her costume-making secrets. You heard right, Tommo. I, Big Bart, will provide you with a disguise tonight. And not even your nearest and dearest friends will be able to recognize you.'

When the sun had set and the cool evening had arrived, Jesus and his disciples made their way to Matthew's house. They came in twos and threes, and last of all came Pip and Tommo and Big Bart.

'This is not going to work,' groaned Tommo. 'I can feel it!'

'I'm sorry, kind stranger, did you say something?' asked Bart. 'And why do you walk so closely to my friend and me?'

'Give it a rest, Bart,' sighed Pip. 'You know perfectly well that it's Tommo.'

'It sounds like Tommo,' Bart agreed. 'But it looks like someone I have never seen before – so amazing is his disguise!'

'I think that's pushing it, big guy,' Pip observed. 'All you gave him was a mudbeard.'

'Ah, but what a beautiful mudbeard it is!' Bart said, proudly. 'Look at the detailed work, the fine curlicues at the end. See, you can pick out every piece of hair!'

'I think I can pick out bits of straw as well,' grumbled Tommo. 'Where did you say you got this mud?'

'Don't pick at it!' Bart scolded. 'You'll ruin the effect.'

'But I can hardly move my mouth,' Tommo complained. 'And it smells kinda funny. Are you sure this is mud?'

'My dear Tommo,' Bart sighed. 'A true artist can fashion a masterpiece from any medium. The source of the mud. What is mixed in the mud. Where I found the mud. Who did what in the mud. All of that is irrelevant. It is only the finished product that counts!'

'Whatever you say,' sighed Tommo. 'Let's just get in there and hope for the best.'

But before they could enter Matthew's house, Pip, Tommo and Big Bart were approached by a couple of religious leaders.

'You there, stop!' called the first religious leader. 'We want to talk to you.'

'That's right, you three!' called the second. 'The big one and the little one. And the one with the mudbeard.'

'I'm worried,' Bart whispered.

'I'm sure it will be fine,' Pip whispered back.

'I am utterly and completely doomed,' whispered Tommo.

'You are Jesus' disciples, are you not?' said the first religious leader, like he was making an accusation.

'That's right,' Pip nodded.

'So why are you and your master eating

at the house of a notorious sinner like Matthew?' asked the second.

'The question had kind of occurred to us as well,' Tommo admitted.

'But we're late for tea,' added Bart.

'So we'll ask – and let you know,' offered Pip.

And they shuffled past the religious leaders and into the house.

They were the last guests to arrive, and so there were only three seats left, bunched together between two of Matthew's friends.

'I'm not sitting next to the goon,' Tommo whispered, as they made their way round the table.

'Goon,' Bart chuckled. 'I do love that word.'

'Then you can sit next to him,' Tommo grunted. 'And Pip can sit next to you. And I will then be as far away from him as possible!'

'Sounds good to me,' said Pip. And they sat themselves down and joined in the meal.

It was an amazing spread. And Bart grinned as he glanced around the table.

'My favourite food groups!' he exclaimed. 'The cake group. The pie group. And the goat group.' And he grabbed himself a handful of each and piled them on his plate. Then he turned to Pip and asked, 'What are you having?'

'A mixture of food I can actually live on,' Pip said. 'You know, the odd vegetable. That sort of thing.'

'Each to his own!' Bart smiled. But when he turned to eat what was on his plate, it was gone!

'Hey!' he shouted. 'Where'd my grub go?' Then he looked at the 'goon' who was sitting next to him. Cake crumbs covered his face, and there was the tip of a crunchy goat tail dangling from his mouth.

'Pip!' Bart whispered. 'Pip! The guy sitting next to me nicked my grub!'

'So tell him to stop it,' Pip shrugged.

'Have you seen the size of him?' Bart said. 'He's three times as big as me! And I remember what Tommo said about that "arm and leg" thing. I like my arms. And my legs.'

'Then just take some more!' Pip said. 'He can't possibly eat all your food!'

Tommo, meanwhile, was keeping his head down and chewing as little as possible, for fear that his mudbeard would crack and fall off. The attractive woman sitting next to him, however, would not let him be.

'You eat like a bird,' she cooed. 'I like that in a man. And I like a nicely trimmed beard, as well!'

'Thank you,' Tommo muttered. 'That's . . . that's very kind.'

'I've never seen a beard like that!' she continued. 'So finely combed. And the smell? What sort of oils do you use?'

'It's a . . . secret mixture,' he answered. 'Courtesy of my friend over there. I'll ask him if you like.'

But Bart had plenty more problems of his own.

'He did it AGAIN!' Bart whispered to Pip. 'He nicked my grub!'

'Well I don't know what you expect me to do?' Pip grumbled. 'If I say something he's likely to eat me, too!'

So Bart tried to keep the goon from touching his food, while Tommo struggled to keep the pretty lady from touching his beard. And by the end of the meal, neither had succeeded.

'GOOD GRUB!' grunted the goon. And he patted Bart on the back, nearly knocking him to the floor.'

'GOOD GRACIOUS!' exclaimed the pretty lady. 'That beard is hard as a rock. You must use some amazing gel!'

And as they left, Pip, Tommo and Big Bart talked together about Matthew's dinner.

'I got really full,' said Pip.

'I got a date!' grinned Tommo.

'I got really hungry,' sighed Bart. 'But then I got a new friend. Seems that his arms were really sore. Apparently that breaking legs thing takes a lot out of you. He thought I was simply getting his food for him, so he wouldn't have to reach so far. He was very grateful. So if WE ever need anybody's legs breaking . . .'

'I don't think that's likely,' said Pip. 'But I'm glad it all worked out for you.'

'And I'm glad that the three of you got on so well with the guests sitting next to you,' said Jesus, who had walked up behind them.

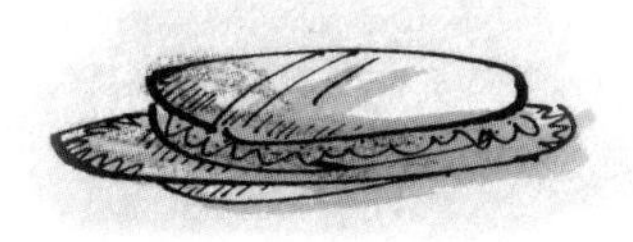

'That reminds me, Jesus,' said Pip. 'We met a couple of religious leaders as we were coming in. They had a question.'

'Yeah,' Bart nodded. 'They wanted to know why you ate with sinners.'

Jesus smiled. 'They would, wouldn't they? How would you answer them?'

'Well, if by sinners,' Bart answered, 'you mean Gordon . . .'

'Gordon?' asked Pip.

'Yeah. Gordon. The goon,' Bart shrugged.

'The goon?' asked Jesus.

'That's what he said his name was. Gordon the Goon. Who was I to argue? Anyway, if by sinners you mean Gordon, then I would say that if I had not talked to him, then I would not have discovered what a nice fellow he was.'

'But he ate all your cakes!' Pip reminded him.

'True,' Bart nodded, 'but I would have probably done the same thing if I had been in his enormous shoes.'

'That's good, Bart,' Jesus grinned. 'I think I would also have said that you send a doctor to somebody who needs to be healed, not to someone who is already well. So if somebody needs a bad habit fixing . . .'

'Like nicking every cake in sight,' Bart suggested.

'Like thievery or gluttony,' Jesus agreed, 'then that's who I am going to spend my time with. Nice mudbeard, by the way, Tommo!'

'Thank you, Jesus,' Tommo sighed.

'Which brings me to Matthew. And his former job. And your former debt.'

'Former?' asked Tommo hopefully.

'That's right,' Jesus smiled. 'You see, what needed fixing in Matthew was his greed, his dishonesty, and his tendency to resort to leg-breaking if he didn't get his way – all of which he has promised to leave behind, now that he is following me.'

'So I'm off the hook?' asked Tommo.

'You're off the hook,' Jesus grinned.

'Which means . . . ?' asked Tommo.

'Which means you can wash off that beard,' Jesus answered, wrinkling his nose. 'Are you sure it's made of mud?'

Chapter 2
Sleep

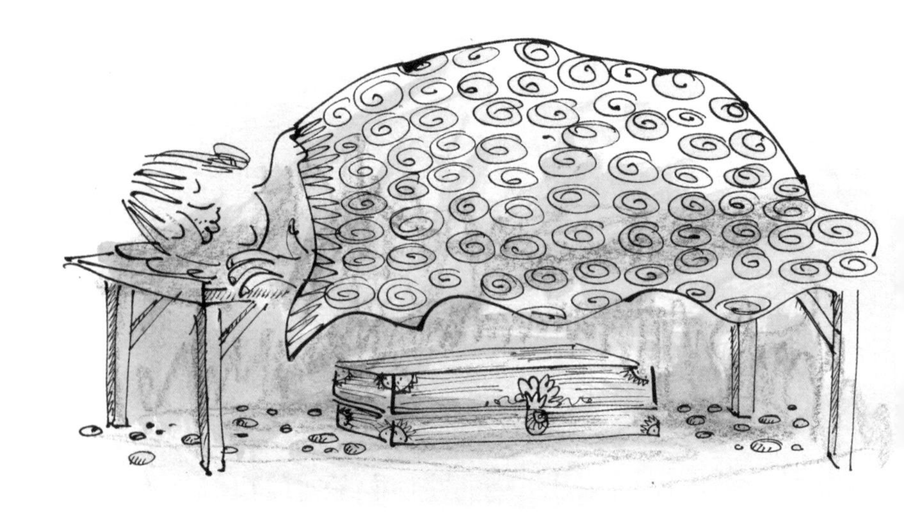

Bart yawned. Bart yawned again. Bart yawned a third time.

'We keeping you up, big man?' Tommo grunted.

'No-aaaaah,' Bart yawned a fourth time. 'I was out with Matthew and some of his mates last night. We got in really late.' Then he yawned a fifth time and stretched his Big Bart arms. 'I just want to go to sleep.'

'There's no time for that,' said Tommo. 'Jesus says we have a really busy day ahead of us. Just keep walking.'

'Can't,' Bart yawned again. 'Need pillow. Need bed. Need one massive long nap!' And he stretched and he yawned one more time, just to make the point.

But Pip reached up and tapped him on the shoulder.

'I think you're gonna have to put that nap on hold, big fella. Look!'

Sure enough, a huge crowd was making its way towards Jesus and his friends.

And at the front of the crowd was a very official-looking man.

'Hey, I know him!' said Pip. 'His name is Jairus. He runs the local synagogue.'

'I could use a synagogue about now,' Bart yawned. 'A little praying. A little preaching. Puts me right to sleep.'

'No, no, he's really good,' Pip objected. 'And he's a friend of my cousin Sam. Used to have us over for dinner all the time. He has a real nice family.'

'Very interesting,' Bart yawned again. 'So interesting that I might just fall asleep where I'm standing.'

As soon as he reached Jesus, Jairus fell to his knees.

'Please help my daughter,' he begged. 'She's only twelve. She's all I've got. And she's dying.'

'Omigosh!' Pip shouted again. 'Did you hear that? Jesus has got to do something!'

And so Jesus did.

'C'mon, lads,' he called to his friends – and they set off straight away, pushing back through the crowd.

'Don't worry,' said Tommo. 'Jesus'll fix it!'

'I sure hope so,' said Pip.

'And then I can have that nap!' added Bart, rubbing his eyes.

But almost as soon as he'd started, Jesus stopped. And he looked round. And he asked a question.

'Who touched me?'

Bart looked at Tommo. Tommo looked at

Pip. Pip looked at Bart. They all looked puzzled, and each of them was thinking exactly the same thing.

Who touched you? A gazillion people – that's who!

But it was Jesus' friend Peter who actually said something.

'Teacher,' he said. 'Look at the crowd. There are people all around you!'

Jesus nodded. 'I know. But this was different. It wasn't a bump or a nudge or any kind of casual contact. Somebody touched me because they needed my help. And I felt the healing power of God flow out of me.'

'Wow!' wowed Tommo. 'That's amazing!'

'Yeah,' added Pip. 'But what about Jairus's daughter?'

'Whaaaat?' yawned Bart. He could hardly keep awake.

'Stay with us, big fella!' said Pip. 'Jesus is doing his miracle thing again. But he'd better hurry.'

'I knoooooow,' Bart yawned once more. 'I'm sooo sleepy. And we still have to go to that synagogue guy's house. I'll never get my nap.'

Just then, a woman fell trembling at Jesus' feet.

'It was me,' she admitted. 'I'm the one who touched you. I've had a problem with

bleeding for twelve years. I've spent all my money on doctors but no one has been able to heal me. Well, not until now. Because when I touched you, the bleeding stopped!'

The crowd cheered. Jesus smiled. Then he took her hand, lifted her to her feet, and said,

'It's your faith – the trust you put in me and in God's power – that has healed you. Go in peace.'

Everyone was happy. Jesus. The woman. The crowd. Everyone but Jairus, who was looking more worried than ever. And Pip.

'C'mon. C'mon!' he whispered. 'We've got to get going.' And then he saw someone pushing through the crowd – pushing right to them.

'Hey,' Pip said, 'that's my cousin! That's Sam!'

And he jumped up and down and shouted and waved.

But Sam paid him no attention.

No attention at all. He was looking straight at Jairus. And his look was not a happy one.

'Jairus,' said Sam, huffing and puffing to catch his breath and trying his best to hold back his tears. 'Your daughter . . .' Sam continued, and he couldn't even bring himself to say her name. 'Your daughter is dead. There's no need for Jesus to come now.'

The whole crowd went quiet. Bart stopped his yawning. And Pip rubbed the corner of one eye.

'You got something stuck in there?' said Bart.

'Can't you see he's upset?' whispered Tommo.

'Shut up. Both of you,' sniffled Pip. And then he sighed and added, 'Jesus heals other people. Stupid naked demon guys. People we don't even know. How come he doesn't heal our friends?'

Jesus looked at Jairus. He was very serious.

'Don't be afraid,' he said. 'Trust me – like that woman did – and your daughter will be healed, too.'

'See?' said Tommo, his hand on Pip's shoulder. 'Jesus is going to heal her.'

'But she's already dead!' Pip sighed. 'That's what Sam said.'

Bart scratched his head, remembering. 'But so was that boy. The one from Nain. He was already in his coffin, and Jesus brought him back from the dead.'

'So maybe he can do the same with the girl!' said Tommo. 'C'mon, let's go.'

Pip and Tommo and Big Bart followed the crowd to Jairus's house. But when they arrived, all they could hear was weeping and wailing.

Bart shook his head sadly. 'Professional mourners. You don't hire them unless you're sure. Looks like Sam was right, Pip. The girl really is dead.'

But Jesus had a different opinion.

'Why all the fuss?' he said to the crowd. 'The girl isn't dead. She's only sleeping.'

And at once the weeping turned into mocking laughter.

'Yeah, right!'

'That's what you say.'

'Pull the other one, Jesus.'

'Uh-oh,' whispered Tommo, 'that didn't go down well.'

'They're upset!' said Pip. 'What do you expect?'

'Sleep,' yawned Bart. 'At least someone gets to sleep.'

And then he scratched his head again.

'So is she really asleep? Or is she dead? Or is she just dead tired? Or is she sleeping the sleep of the dead? Or is Jesus just saying she's asleep, because she's really dead and . . . and . . .'

'And he means to wake her up!' grinned Tommo. 'Like he did with the boy from Nain.'

'That's what I'm hoping,' said Pip, softly. 'But it's a lot to hope for.'

'Then let's go and see!' said Bart.

But before they could step into the house, Jesus pointed at Peter, James and John.

'You three,' he said. 'Come with me. The rest of you – stay out here.' And along with Jairus and his wife, Jesus and Peter and James and John went into the house.

'Flippin' fishermen!' grumbled Tommo. 'They always get the best jobs.'

'Peter, James and John. Teacher's pets,' moaned Bart.

'Sam!' shouted Pip. 'Over here!' And his cousin saw him and came running and gave him a big hug.

Amazingly, he was almost exactly as tall as Pip – which wasn't very tall at all. They could have been twins. In fact, except that Sam was . . .

'Hairier,' observed Bart. 'You look a lot like Pip, except you're a whole lot hairier.'

'It's from my mother's side,' chuckled Sam, in a voice much like Pip's, as well. 'Hairy heads. Hairy beards. Hairy arms. And look, we've even got hair on our toes!'

'Impressive,' grunted Tommo, but he didn't sound impressed at all. 'Oh, and sorry about your friend.'

'Mary?' Sam sighed. 'Yeah. I sure hope Jesus can do something. But, to be honest, I think it's too late.' And then he started rubbing the corner of his eye, much like Pip had done earlier.

'We were inseparable when we were kids. Pip'll tell you. Mary was younger, yeah, but she was a bit of a tomboy and followed us wherever we went.'

And Pip just nodded and sighed. 'Sam, Mary and Pip. What adventures we had!'

'I wish we could go in there and see what's happening,' said Bart.

'Jesus told us not to,' Tommo reminded him.

'But he didn't tell me,' grinned Sam. 'There's a window round the back. It's kind of high off the ground, but if someone could give me a leg up . . .' And he looked at Bart and winked.

'Yeah, that would be handy . . .' Bart mused. And then the denarius dropped. 'Oh, you mean me? Yeah. Sure.'

'We can all help!' offered Pip. 'If you promise to tell us what you see in there.'

So, forming a sort of human set of steps, Pip, then Tommo, then Bart kneeled, all-fours, on the ground. And Sam bounded up on their backs, one-two-three, and peeped his hairy head above the window sill.

'They're all in the room,' he whispered to Bart, who passed the message on. 'Jesus' back is to me. He's leaning over the bed. I'm looking straight at Mary and she's just lying there. She doesn't look good. Now Jesus is taking her hand. And he's saying something.

Sounds like . . . sounds like . . . "Little girl, get up!" And she is! I mean, she's up! She's awake! She's not dead!'

Pip jumped up for joy. And so did Tommo. And so did Big Bart, too! And Sam, of course, who was still on Bart's back went shooting up into the air and past the window and caught

Mary's eye on the way down. And she laughed at the sight of her friend flying by but no one else inside was any the wiser because they were so happy that she was alive!

A slap-up meal followed. It was Jesus' idea, the theory being that dying and coming back to life works up quite an appetite.

But when everyone gathered round the table, one of the seats was empty.

'Where's Bart?' asked Jesus. 'Can't imagine him missing a meal.'

And then they heard something.

Something out the back. Something that sounded like someone snoring. And when Pip and Tommo and Sam looked out the back window, there was Bart, his back propped up against the house, his head lolling to one side and his mouth wide open.

'Looks like he's asleep,' observed Pip.

'Looks like he's dead,' grunted Tommo.

'Dead? Asleep?' grinned Sam. 'When Jesus is around, it doesn't seem to matter!'

Chapter 3

Food

'What was that?' Tommo grunted.

'What?' asked Bart.

'That noise?'

Bart shrugged. 'I didn't hear anything.'

'Well I did,' said Pip. 'It sounded like a wolf. A wolf devouring a sheep.'

'Or maybe strangling it,' noted Tommo. 'Yeah. Definitely. Strangling. A ravenous wolf and a strangled sheep.'

'And a duck,' Pip added. 'I think I heard a duck as well. A deranged duck, with one mad eye, as it smacks into a tree.'

'Hmm,' Bart

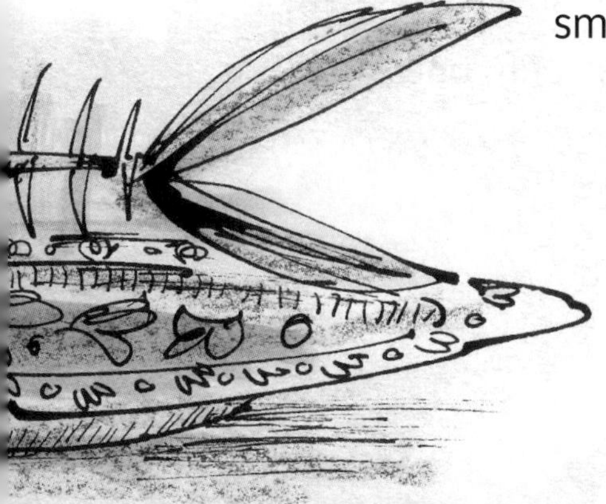

nodded. 'A ravenous wolf. A strangled sheep. A deranged duck. That would be my stomach. I'm famished!'

'Me, too,' sighed Pip.

'Well, we've been here all day!' said Tommo. 'Jesus has taught some good stuff. And he's healed people. It takes time. What do you expect?'

'A lunch break!' said Bart. 'But then, I didn't actually bring any lunch.'

'I don't think anybody did,' observed Pip. 'Listen, there are plenty more deranged ducks and strangled sheep out there in the crowd. We aren't the only ones who are hungry.'

'Makes you think about food, though, doesn't it?' said Tommo, dreamily. 'Like a big pot of lamb stew.'

'Stop it!' cried Bart, shoving his fingers into his ears.

'Makes you even hungrier, doesn't it, big fella?' grinned Pip.

'No, it makes me ILL!' Big Bart choked. 'The lumpy lamby bits get stuck in your throat and make you gag! It's horrible!'

'So I guess it's chicken stew for you, then,' suggested Tommo.

Bart turned green. 'Chicken stew!' he cringed. 'That's even worse! When she was expecting me, my mum was frightened by a rabid rooster. I get hives if I even smell a chicken.'

'Wow!' said Pip. 'I did not know that. I have obviously not been paying attention to your diet. So you're a vegetarian, then?'

And Bart just howled. 'Veggies? Nooooo! I can't stand veggies. And there's a broccoli-shaped rash on my bum to prove it!'

'So what can you eat, big fella?' Tommo asked.

'Cakes, mostly,' Bart smiled. 'And pies. And sweets. And goat-on-a-stick.'

'Well, that explains the belly, doesn't it?' Tommo sighed.

'Hey! I'm big-boned,' Bart protested.

'And big-bottomed,' chuckled Pip. 'Sorry!'

Just then, Jesus walked by.

'The crowd's getting hungry, lads,' he said.

'You can almost hear their stomachs grumbling.'

'Ravenous wolves,' muttered Tommo.

'Strangled sheep,' added Pip.

'Something about one-eyed ducks,' Bart concluded.

'If you say so,' shrugged Jesus. 'But the question is, where are we going to buy food for all of them?'

'Buy food?' Pip sniggered. 'For this lot? It's just a guess, but I reckon it would cost something like eight months' wages!'

'And that's on good pay,' added Tommo, 'with overtime.'

'And even then,' Bart concluded, 'no one would get more than an itsy-bitsy, teeny-weeny, bite-sized little bit. There's no way we can feed all these people. It's a joke, right?'

But Jesus wasn't laughing.

'Just thought it would be helpful for us to understand the scale of the problem,' he grinned.

'And . . . ?' asked Pip.

'And here's Andrew,' Jesus announced, 'with the beginning of a solution!'

Andrew had a boy with him. The boy had a basket. And in the basket were five small loaves of barley bread and two little fish.

'It's not much of a beginning,' shrugged Tommo.

'No,' Jesus smiled. 'But then neither was the water in those jars before I turned it into wine.'

'Point taken,' said Tommo. 'So you're going to turn the fish and bread into . . . ?'

'More fish and bread, I think,' said Jesus. And he bowed his head and said, 'Thank you for this food, Father. Make it enough to feed

this crowd. Teach us to share and help us to see that, with your help, there is always more than enough to go around.'

Then he opened his eyes and started breaking off chunks of fish and bread. And the more he broke off, the more there was!

'That's amazing!' cried Tommo.

'Another miracle!' shouted Pip.

But Bart just sat there shaking and shivering . . . and scratching.

'Fish-itch. Fish-itch. Fish-itch,' he repeated, over and over again.

'Sorry, Jesus,' Pip apologized. 'Bart has a whole mess of dietary issues. It looks like he's allergic to fish as well.'

'No problem,' said Jesus. 'You two help the others pass out the food, and I'll find something else for Bart to do.'

So Pip and Tommo grabbed as much fish and bread as they could carry and started passing it round. Up and down and back and forth across the hillside they went. And the crowd was thrilled!

Bart, meanwhile, was sent to talk to one of Jesus' other disciples, Matthew, who gave him a fish-free assignment. And that's what he was doing when Pip and Tommo came back for another load of food.

'So what are you up to, big fella?' asked Pip.

'A completely impossible job,' Bart sighed, 'that's what.'

'Well, at least you're not itching,' said Tommo.

'No, but my head hurts,' Bart moaned. 'You know how Matthew is always writing stuff down – what we do and what Jesus says. Well, he thinks it would be helpful if we knew how many people were being fed today.'

'There are gazillions!' said Pip.

'That's what I told him,' Bart explained. 'But he said "gazillions" wasn't a real number. He wanted me to make a REAL count, with PROPER numbers – so he'd know exactly how many there were.'

'That's rough,' Tommo grunted.

'You're telling me,' Bart sighed again. 'I started with the kids. But they take a bite and then they run around. So they're here, they're there. You don't know if you counted the same kid once or twice or six times! And their mums are no better. They keep running after them, shouting at them to finish their lunch.'

'So just count the men,' Pip suggested. 'They're all sitting down, nice and still, stuffing their faces. That'll be easy. And then just say there were some women and children, too.'

A huge smile broke out across Bart's face.

'Pip, you are a genius! I would give you a big hug, except that you smell like fish and even from here you are starting to make me retch.'

'Fair enough, big fella,' Pip grinned. 'Looks like there's another load of grub to pass round anyway. Jesus just keeps breaking off more. His fingers must be getting really tired! We'll see you when it's all over.'

So they all went back to work, and when everyone had been fed, and twelve whole baskets full of leftovers had been collected, Pip, Tommo and Big Bart collapsed on the hillside.

'I'm shattered,' said Pip.

'Totally and completely exhausted,' Tommo agreed.

'My brain hurts,' added Bart. 'And my fingers and my toes. I never knew counting could be so hard.'

'So what's the final number?' asked Pip.

'Four thousand, nine hundred and eighty-seven,' sighed Bart. 'Best as I can figure.'

'Well at least Matthew will be pleased,' Tommo grunted.

'Don't think so,' said Bart. 'I mean he's writing this stuff down, so I guess he wants to make it into a book someday. But it just doesn't sound good, does it – "The Feeding of the 4,987"?'

'So round it up,' suggested Pip. 'Who will know?'

'Another genius idea!' Bart beamed. '"The Feeding of the 4,990". It has a ring to it!'

And then he hopped to his Big Bart feet.

'Where you going?' asked Tommo.

'To tell Matthew,' said Bart. And he trundled up over the crest of the hill. But no sooner had he gone than he was back again, with a boy in tow.

'Look what I found!' he shouted.

'Another boy?' asked Tommo.

'With another basket?' added Pip.

'Exactly!' grinned Bart. 'But he doesn't have fish and bread in his basket. Look!' And he flung it open. 'Cakes!'

'So you're off to see Jesus, aren't you?' sighed Tommo.

'You betcha!' Bart grinned. 'This miracle isn't over. Not by a long shot. There are 4,990 people out there who need some pudding!'

Chapter 4
Water

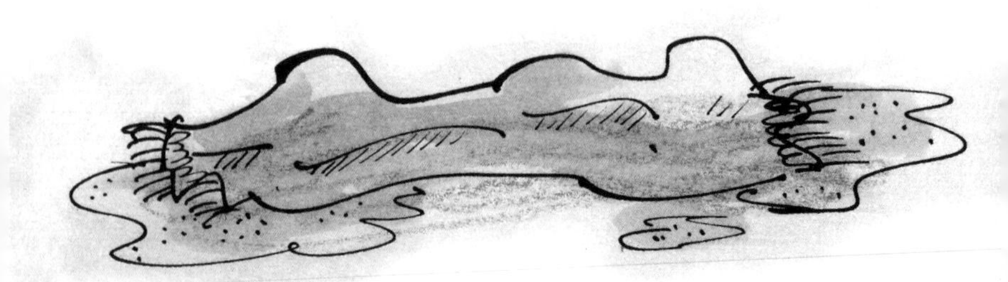

Big Bart crossed his arms and stood stock still, like an enormous statue.

'I'm not going,' he grunted. 'Don't ask me again.'

'But the boat is ready to go!' sighed Pip. 'Everyone's waiting.'

'Don't care,' muttered Bart. 'Not going.'

'Chicken,' clucked Tommo.

'Not going.'

'Cluck-cluck-cluck!' added Pip.

'Still not going.'

'Big girl's tunic!' tried Tommo.

'Sticks and stones. Not going. NOT going. NOT GOING!'

'Stop it!' Pip shouted. 'Stop it right now! Are we going to have this exact same conversation *every* time we have to get into a boat?'

'Umm . . . maybe,' Bart muttered.

'But it went fine the last time,' argued Tommo.

'Apart from the fact that I puked up both my breakfast and my lunch, sure,' Bart reminded him. 'Oh, and there was the little matter of that storm. The one that almost KILLED us.'

'But Jesus made the storm go away,' countered Pip.

'And Jesus won't be going with us this time, will he?' Bart protested. 'He told us to get into the boat and cross the lake, and that he was going up the mountainside to pray. Which means that if there is another storm, we will all be doomed! And besides,' he added, 'I'm hungry.'

'And whose fault is that?' moaned Tommo. 'Jesus just fed 5,000 people!'

'4,987 to be precise,' said Bart.

'The point is that there was plenty of food to go around,' Pip argued. 'Fish and bread for everyone!'

'As I have explained,' Bart explained, 'I am allergic to fish. And I don't like the little crunchy bits in that kind of bread. Now, if it had been a different kind of bread . . .'

'If it had been a different kind of bread,' Tommo sighed, 'you would have found something wrong with that as well! If you weren't so flippin' finicky, you'd be full like the rest of us!'

'That's not fair,' Bart reprimanded him. 'There were those cakes that belonged to that other little boy, which I would have gladly eaten. But when I asked Jesus to break them up and pass them round, too, he just laughed. I think he thought I was joking. But I wasn't.'

'Because you wanted those cakes, didn't you, big fella?' Pip grinned.

'I did,' sighed Bart. 'I really did.'

'Well, it just so happens,' Pip continued, 'that I was looking out for you. I had a word with that boy. He gave me a couple of those cakes. And they are in my bag, at this very moment!'

'That was very thoughtful,' Bart grinned back. 'May I have them, please?'

'Sure,' said Pip. And he tossed the bag in Bart's direction. Or, more precisely, he threw the bag high over Bart's head and past his grasping hands. It sailed through the air and landed in the back of the boat. And like a puppy in pursuit of a ball or a bone, Bart followed the bag, heedless of his surroundings, and finished up in the boat as well!

Pip and Tommo hopped aboard and shouted, 'Shove off!' And with Bart's head buried in the bag, they set sail across the lake.

It was only when he came up for air, mouth full and face covered with crumbs, that Bart realized what had happened.

'Not fair!' he sputtered, bits of cake spewing out in every direction. 'You tricked me!'

'Yes,' Pip admitted. 'But at least you got your cakes.'

'I'll say,' grunted Tommo. 'I've never seen food go down so fast.'

And then the boat hit a bumpy wave. And then another and then a third. And Bart turned green.

'I think it might be coming back even faster,' he gulped. And with a 'Hwork!' he deposited what no longer looked much like

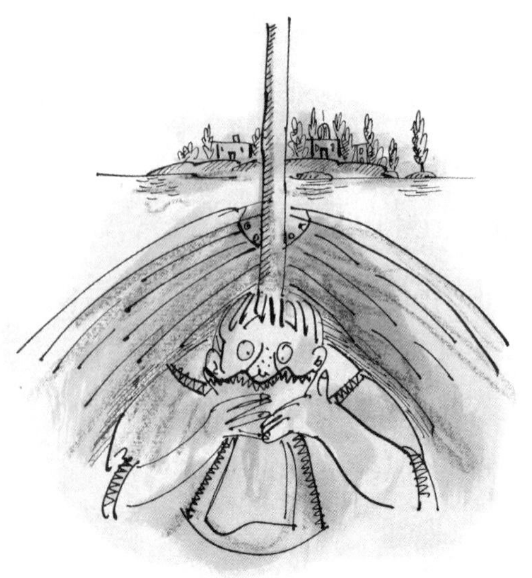

cakes back in the bottom of Pip's bag!

'That's my bag!' Pip cried.

'That's disgusting!' Tommo grunted.

'That's hilarious!' Peter howled. 'He's lost his lunch again!' And Andrew and James and John laughed along with him.

'Shut up!' Pip shouted. 'He isn't like you lot. He hasn't spent his whole life on a boat!'

And Tommo just shook his head and muttered, 'Flippin' fishermen!'

'Sorry,' Peter chuckled. 'We'll try to be more understanding. It's just that he has no idea how bad it can really get out here.'

'I'll say!' added Andrew. 'Do you remember that wave a few years back? The one that looked like a tunnel? We got through it just before it collapsed.'

'Or the night the mast split right in half,' said John.

'Or the time old Ebenezer got knocked off the back of the boat,' James went on. 'He was coughing up crayfish for a month!'

And then they all laughed out loud again.

'That's enough!' Pip shouted.

'Can't you see you're making things worse?' grumbled Tommo. 'Why don't you just leave us alone and go back to your . . . your . . . flippin' fisherman stuff?'

And Bart just sat there whimpering, fingers jammed in his ears, repeating over and over again, 'Happy thoughts. Happy thoughts. Cakes. Happy thoughts.'

Pip patted him on the head. 'Hang in there, big fella.'

And Tommo put a hand on his shoulder. 'It'll be all right, mate.'

But it wasn't. Not by a long shot.

The sun set. The moon rose. And then the clouds rolled in. The further they sailed, the harder the wind blew. And the more difficult it got to make any progress at all.

'Looks like we're in for a rough night!' called Peter.

'Hold on, everybody,' added Andrew, 'it's going to get bumpy!'

'And that means you, Landlubber Bart!' shouted John.

'You mean land-blubberer,' sniggered his brother James.

Pip staggered to his feet, ready to shout right back, determined to shut them up. But there was no need. The fishermen had already fallen silent. They were looking past him, across the water. They were pointing. And they were trembling.

'What is it?' croaked Peter.

'Too small for a boat,' Andrew shivered.

'Too big for a fish,' quivered John.

'That's 'cause it's a person,' squeaked James, as the clouds parted and the moonlight shone on the mysterious figure. 'It's not a "something" out there. It's a "somebody". It's a ghost!'

So frightened were the fishermen, that Pip started to tremble, too. But he had to have a look. He just had to. Slowly he turned round, his fingers like a fence in front of his face, one eye shut and the other peeping through the tiniest finger-fence gap.

He looked. He saw. He screamed. And then he jumped back down to where he'd been sitting and burrowed as best he could behind Bart.

'It's true!' he trembled. 'It's out there, on the water. And it's coming straight for us. A ghost!'

'A ghost!' said Bart. And he opened his eyes and sat up straight, as a Big Bart smile crossed his no-longer-frightened face. 'I love ghosts!'

'You mean, you've seen one?' stammered Tommo. 'You've seen a ghost?'

'Well, not exactly. But my Uncle Jeroboam did and I have been dying to see one, myself, ever since. You see, he came home from a wedding party, once – a little worse for wear, if you know what I mean – and he tried to milk

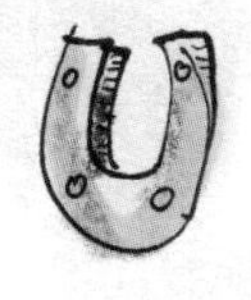
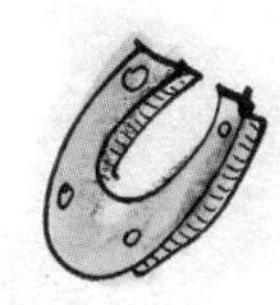

the donkey. The donkey was not impressed and kicked Uncle Jeroboam across the yard. He was unconscious for a long while, but when he woke up, there was the ghost!

'"Jeroboam!" the ghost called in what my uncle says was a terrifying, high, shrieking voice. "Forsake your wicked ways. Do not indulge in much wine!" And then he passed out again.

'It's all very spooky, and what makes things even more strange is that he says the ghost looked exactly like Aunt Agatha. Who died. Two years later.'

'Not to be sceptical,' Tommo said, unwilling to let even mortal dread keep him from puncturing Bart's tale. 'But seeing as your aunt died two years later, is it not possible that the ghost actually was . . .'

'Look!' cried Bart, leaping to his feet. 'I see it! I see it. There it is!'

And then he waved. 'Hello, Ghosty! Nice to meet you! Why don't you come and join us?'

And, as one, the rest of the disciples cried, 'NO!!!'

But the ghost did exactly what Bart asked and moved step by watery step towards the bouncing boat.

'Get us out of here!' shouted Andrew.

'It's no use,' Peter shouted back. 'Can't make any headway. The wind's too strong. We're stuck!'

Head buried in hands, John cried out as well, 'If only Jesus were here, he'd know what to do!'

'As it happens,' said Bart, holding a finger in the air. 'I think he is. That ghost doesn't look like Aunt Agatha at all. It looks like Jesus!'

And with that, a familiar and friendly voice called out across the waves.

'Have courage, lads! Don't be afraid. It's only me.'

Slowly, each of the disciples lifted up his head and looked.

'I think Bart's right,' said Andrew.

'I think it's really him,' said John.

'I think I wet myself,' sighed James.

'I think I'm going to join him!' announced Peter. And he leapt right into a passing wave.

'NO!!!' the disciples cried again.

The wave washed by Peter, and when it had, he was standing on the water, just like Jesus! Slowly they moved towards each other, like they were walking on solid ground. But then the wind began to blow again, and Peter lost his nerve and began to sink.

'Help me, Jesus!' he cried. 'Save me!'

'Who's the blubberer, now?' muttered Tommo. 'Flippin' Peter, that's who.'

But all Jesus said was, 'Why did you stop trusting me? With a little more faith, you could have done it!'

Then he held out his hand and

helped Peter back into the boat. Jesus stepped on board as well. And as soon as he did, the wind stopped its blowing and the waves their bouncing up and down.

Everyone cheered. Everyone but Tommo who was still moaning about 'fishermen', and Bart who looked just a little disappointed.

'What's the matter, big fella?' asked Pip.

'Aww, it's just that I was really looking forward to seeing a ghost, that's all,' Bart sighed.

'But, Bart!' Pip cried. 'You saw Jesus WALKING ON THE WATER! I'd say that's pretty impressive, too.'

'S'pose so,' Bart admitted.

'It's more than that. It's amazing!' said Pip. 'To think that our teacher, our friend, can do stuff like that!'

'Yeah,' Tommo agreed. 'In the last couple of days, he's healed a woman, raised a dead girl and turned a few chunks of fish and bread into a feast. And now this! I'd say that's more than any ordinary teacher could do.'

'I'd say that's the kind of thing you'd only expect God to do!' Pip nodded.

'Or somebody a lot like him,' said Tommo. 'Like his son.'

'Or . . .or . . . his nephew!' added Bart. 'Like if I had seen a ghost – then I would be just the same as my Uncle Jeroboam!'

'Once again,' Tommo interrupted, 'could I point out that your uncle actually didn't . . .'

But before he could finish, Peter shouted, 'Shove off!' And the sails filled up and the boat took off and the sudden jolt knocked the best mates back onto the floor. And, when he'd finished rubbing his head, all Tommo had left to say was, 'Flippin' fishermen!'

Chapter 5
Goat

'I'm exhausted!' Bart sighed.

'That's what you keep telling us,' grunted Tommo.

'My feet hurt!' Bart moaned.

'Heard that, too,' muttered Pip.

'When are we going to . . . ?'

'ENOUGH!' Pip and Tommo shouted, as one.

'We told you to stop asking,' said Tommo.

'We told you the last time you brought it up,' added Pip.

'WE DO NOT KNOW WHEN WE ARE GOING TO GET THERE!' they shouted together again.

'Ha!' Bart laughed. And then he laughed a second time. 'Ha! That's not what I was going to ask. So there!'

'Then what were you going to ask?' Tommo sneered.

'Ummm . . . When are . . . When are we . . . When are we . . . ?' Bart tried his best to come up with a different question. He tried until his brain hurt as much as his big flat feet.

'I got it! When are we going to know where we are going . . . to?'

'We already know!' Tommo sighed. 'Jesus told us before we set off. We're going to

Caesarea Philippi!'

'See, that's my problem,' said Bart. 'I can't get my head around that name! It's too big. Too complicated.'

'Then break it down,' said Pip. 'It starts with Caesar – like the guy who runs the Roman Empire.'

'Caesar. Got it,' Bart nodded.

'And then there's a little ending – ea,' Pip explained. 'Like . . . like . . .'

'Diarrhoea!' Bart suggested.

'All right,' Pip sighed. 'Diarrhoea.'

'So it's Caesar-ea,' said Bart. 'And then . . . ?

'Philip,' said Pip. 'Like my real name.'

'Your real name is Philip?' said Bart,

amazed. 'I did not know that! I always thought that Pip was short for Pippin. Or Pippi. Or Pippopotamus.' And then he put one finger to his chin, considering the situation. 'Philip? Hmm.'

'And then just add "pie",' said Pip. 'Like I was in a pie. Like a Philip-pie. Philippi!'

Bart smiled. 'I like pie. But I like fruit in my pie. Or goat. I think that if I ate a Philip-pie it would make me ill. I'd probably end up with a horrible disease – like Caesar-ea.'

'So have you got it?' asked Tommo.

'I think so,' Bart answered. 'We are going to Caesarea Philippi!' And then he added, 'So when are we going to get there?'

But before Tommo and Pip could tell him to 'stop asking' yet again, Jesus held up his hand and said, 'I've got a question. Something for you to think about while we walk.'

'Excellent!' Bart whispered. 'A quiz! That'll pass the time. I spy with my little eye, something that begins wiiiiith . . . F.'

Tommo whispered back, 'I don't think that's what Jesus has in mind.'

'But it's a good question,' answered Bart. 'Go on, see if you can figure it out.'

'I don't know,' sighed Tommo, looking around. 'Fig tree? Fountain? Fork in the road?'

Bart giggled and pointed at Pip. 'No, it's him! PHILIP!'

'But Philip doesn't begin with . . . oh, never mind,' groaned Pip.

'I said, I have a question,' Jesus repeated. 'Assuming everyone is listening . . .'

And Bart turned to Pip and went, 'Shhh!'

'We've been travelling round together for a while, now,' Jesus continued. 'You've listened to me teach. You've seen the miracles. And you've talked with the people in the places we've visited. So what do they think we're up to? Who do they think I am?'

There was a long pause. And a lot of humming and hawing and head-scratching.

And then they walked past a street vendor.

'Oooh, look!' Bart whispered. 'He's selling food. He's got goat-on-a-stick! That's my favourite.'

'But we're supposed to be thinking about the question,' Pip protested.

'I don't know the answer,' Bart shrugged. 'And I don't talk to anybody but you two. And myself, occasionally. So I'm not likely to be of any help.

'But what I do know is that I'm hungry and I'm tired. So I'll just stay behind and have a little goaty treat, then catch up with you in a bit. OK?'

And before they could say 'No!' or 'Don't!' or 'Hang on a minute!' Bart had slipped away.

'Got to admit,' admitted Tommo, 'I don't know the answer either.'

But James did. He put up his hand and he spoke.

'Some people think you're John the Baptist.'

'That's a bit of a stretch,' whispered Tommo to Pip. 'John the Baptist is dead.'

But Jesus had very good hearing!

'You're right, Tommo,' he nodded. 'John is dead. Executed by King Herod because he dared to criticize the king's behaviour. You can get into trouble when you stand up against what's wrong.'

Jesus looked very sad.

'He was my cousin, you know, on my mum's side. Just six months older than me.

Sent by God to tell the world that I was coming. I miss him.'

Everything went quiet for a bit, and then someone else put his hand up. It was Thaddeus.

'Some people say you're a prophet, Jesus. Elijah, maybe.'

Jesus smiled. 'A prophet. God's messenger. And Elijah was a good one. A bit like John, in a way – standing up for what was right against another evil and corrupt king – a long, long time ago.'

'He went to heaven in a fiery chariot, didn't he?' asked Pip.

'So he did,' Jesus grinned. 'And I suppose that's why people think I might be him – Elijah come back again! It's a better guess, but hey, if I had a chariot of fire, we wouldn't have to do all this walking! So I think it will have to be "no" to that one as well.'

Everybody chuckled, and then there were more suggestions – Jeremiah or one of the other prophets.

'Look,' Jesus said at last, 'it's interesting to hear what other people have to say, but I suppose the more important question is this: Who do YOU think that I am?'

Things went quiet again. And that was followed by a lot more whispering.

'Not sure what to say,' whispered Pip.

'Well, you know what I think,' Tommo whispered back.

'You said it from the start,' Pip answered. 'You think he's the Messiah, right?'

Tommo nodded. 'The Special One. The Chosen One. Sent by God to defeat the Romans and give us back our land again. That's what I'm hoping for, anyway.'

Pip scratched his head. 'But there's more to him than that,' he said. 'He does things we never heard that the Messiah would do. He feeds thousands of people with a boy's lunch. He stills storms. He walks on water! That's more than Messiah stuff. That's God stuff! But, he can't possibly be . . .'

And that's when Bart returned.

'Greetings, lads!' he said. 'And look at what I've got. Not one, not two, but three supersize portions of goat-on-a-stick. And an extra large bottle of goat juice, to boot! Never say that your buddy Bart doesn't know how to take care of his friends.'

And then he passed them round. 'One for Tommo. One for . . . PHILIP.'

'That's nice, Bart. Thanks,' said Pip. 'But we're kind of busy right now. Jesus just changed the question.'

'Yeah,' Tommo added. 'He wants to know who WE think he is.'

'Well, why didn't he ask that in the first place?' Bart shrugged. 'It's obvious, isn't it? He's the Messiah. And the Son of God.'

'Well, say something, then!' spluttered Pip.

'Put your hand up,' said Tommo, grabbing Bart's arm and hoisting it in the air.'

'Careful,' said Bart. 'You'll spill the goat juice!'

And that's when Peter spoke.

'You are the Messiah,' he announced. 'The son of the living God.'

'Hey, that's what I said,' Bart whispered.

'I know. I know,' nodded Pip.

'Flippin' fishermen,' grumbled Tommo.

But Jesus was really pleased. He told Peter that he was right. And he said a lot of nice things about Peter, as well.

'Listen to that!' Tommo groaned. 'Sounds like he's putting Peter in charge of the rest of us.'

'Yeah, that could have been you, big fella,' sighed Pip.

'Doesn't bother me,' Bart shrugged. 'I don't think I'm cut out for that sort of thing. And besides, I've got something Peter hasn't got.'

'What's that, big fella?' asked Tommo.

And Bart grinned and held his lunch high. 'Goat-on-a-stick!'

Chapter 6
Butterfly

Pip, Tommo and Big Bart lay on the mountainside, hands behind their heads, staring up into the sky.

'Ahhh!' Bart sighed happily. 'Rest, at last.'

'Couldn't agree with you more, big guy,' said Tommo.

'A well-deserved holiday, if there ever was one,' Pip agreed.

And then he started to wiggle and wriggle and yelp. And finally he jumped to his feet and started scratching.

'There's something biting me! A bug. A beetle. Get it off! Get it off!'

'Calm down, my little friend,' said Bart. 'It's only a spider. There – on the back of your neck. Got it!'

And Bart plucked it off Pip and held it, dangling in front of his own face.

'Kill it! Kill it!' Pip cried.

'No!' said Bart protectively. 'It's lovely!'

'And possibly poisonous,' observed Tommo. 'I'm with Pip on this one.'

'I am not going to kill it,' Bart insisted. 'I think spiders are amazing. Eight little legs. A headful of eyeballs. And all that incredible web-making equipment. I love 'em!'

Then he set the spider on his forehead, and it crawled away into his hair.

Pip cringed. 'That's disgusting!'

'And potentially life threatening!' added Tommo.

'Nonsense,' Bart shrugged. 'I have never been bitten by a spider in my life. Or any other bug, for that matter.'

'There's a first time for everything,' said Tommo.

'Not for me,' said Bart. 'I love those little critters, and they know it. That's why they leave me alone.'

'Yeah, they're too busy burrowing into your scalp,' winced Pip.

'That is not a burrowing spider,' Bart explained. 'So there is nothing to worry about. I know, because, as you may have observed, I am a keen student of all things buggy.'

'You certainly know how to "bug" us!' Tommo grunted.

'Laugh all you like,' Bart answered. 'Anyone who knows me will tell you. Bugs are my speciality. Ask my Aunt Gomer.'

'How many aunts do you have, exactly?' Pip asked.

'Plenty,' Bart noted.

'But my extensive family is not the point. During the summers I would spend weeks at a time with Aunt Gomer. She was a small, wiry woman with a face like a hedgehog. Disturbing . . . But she had a lovely disposition. Uncle Hosea adored her. He had this curious pet name for her: 'My Little Tiggiwinkle'. It was she who fostered my passion for insects. She would point them out to me as we walked together or foraged for nuts in the undergrowth.'

'You foraged for nuts?' asked Tommo.

'It was a hard time,' Bart remembered. 'And she liked nuts. And grubs. Anyway, she would show me the different insects and then send me out to collect them. And I would always return, the sun setting at the end of the day, with bugs in my hand or on my head or any place I could store them. I remember one time in particular . . .

'"Barty," she said to me, "settle down and stop your jumping about. You act like you have ants in your pants!"

'And I did.'

Just then, Jesus made an announcement. 'I'm going up the mountain, and I need three of you to come with me. Peter, James and John – how about you?'

'There they go again,' Bart sighed. 'If only I had put my hand up and answered Jesus' question, it could have been us.'

'Go on, Tommo,' said Pip. 'Say it. I know you want to.'

'Nah,' Tommo grunted. 'If they want to go traipsing up a mountain while the rest of us relax, that's their business . . . Flippin' fishermen.'

'Ooh, look!' Bart interrupted. 'Did you see that?'

'See what, big fella?' Pip shrugged.

'That butterfly!' Bart exclaimed. 'It just fluttered by my head. It was amazing!'

'Sorry,' said Pip. 'Missed it. Had my eyes shut.'

'Me, too,' added Tommo, yawning. 'But we'll take your word for it. It was a butterfly. It was amazing. Now for that little nap.'

'But you don't understand!' Bart continued. 'That was no ordinary amazing butterfly. That was a "Dead Man's Bottom"!'

'Dead Man's Bottom?' asked Pip.

'So called because the markings on its wings bear a striking resemblance to a sailor who has fallen out of his boat and is left floating, bottom up, in the middle of the Dead Sea!'

'Now that's a pretty picture,' grunted Tommo.

'Do sailors even sail boats on the Dead Sea?' wondered Pip.

'And aren't we miles away from there, anyway?' added Tommo.

'Exactly!' Bart cried. 'That's what makes this so special. And that's why we have to follow it!'

'To catch it?' suggested Pip.

'To kill it?' asked Tommo.

'No!' Bart cried. 'To give it a little pat on the head. It's lovely! Anything else would be cruel.'

'If I was a butterfly,' said Tommo, 'I wouldn't want you patting me on the head.'

'If I was a butterfly,' said Pip, 'I wouldn't want you anywhere near me.'

'If I was a butterfly,' said Bart, looking

wistfully at the sky, 'I'd thank the Lord for giving me wings.' And then he added, 'C'mon, if we hurry we can still find it.'

'I think I'll just hang out here for a while,' yawned Pip.

'Yeah, knock yourself out, big guy,' yawned Tommo, too. 'Let us know how it all turns out.'

'But I need your help,' Bart pleaded. 'Patting a Dead Man's Bottom is not as easy as it sounds.'

'Not when you put it that way,' groaned Pip. 'But I'm still not going.'

'Not even if the spider that is on my head decides to find a new home?' Bart suggested, running his fingers through his hair and pulling out the squiggling creature.

'There you go, little fella. Seems that my buddy Pip would like you to visit him for a while.'

Pip cringed. 'Keep that thing away from me, Bart! I'm warning you . . .'

Bart held the spider to his own ear. 'But he says he's lonely. He wants a new home . . . on Pip Street!'

'That is not funny!' Pip cried.

'What's that, Mr Spider?' Bart went on. 'You say you can't move to Pip Street if Pip Street moves up the mountain? I see!'

'All right, I'm coming. I'm coming,' moaned Pip, struggling to his feet.

'Now he wants to go to Tommo Lane!' Bart grinned.

'Yeah. Yeah. Yeah,' moaned Tommo. 'I get the picture. And as I'm not getting any sleep anyway . . .'

'That's the spirit!' Bart grinned again. Then he dropped the spider back onto his head and said, 'Back on top of Bart Manor, my little friend.'

And the three of them set off after the butterfly.

They climbed for ten minutes, then fifteen. The mountainside was steep.

'This is a waste of time,' Tommo complained.

'There're no amazing butterflies here. Or anything else amazing to look at, for that matter. Just rocks and dirt and scraggly brown shrubs.'

'Let's go back, Bart!' pleaded Pip. 'We're never gonna find that butterfly again. It was a fluke.'

But Bart would not be persuaded. 'We will see that Dead Man's Bottom again,' he assured them. 'I promise. And what a special moment that will be!'

And then Pip stopped. And gasped. 'I do not believe it. Look! There's your butterfly!'

Sure enough, there it was, fluttering about in a clump of ragged bushes.

Bart was ecstatic!

'My Dead Man's Bottom. My Dead Man's Bottom!' he cried. And he launched his oversized self in the general direction of the shrubbery.

Pip and Tommo wandered away, desperate for a little rest.

'That oughta keep him busy for a while,' Tommo whispered.

'Let's hope so,' said Pip. And then he gasped again.

'Not another flippin' butterfly?' moaned Tommo.

'No,' Pip whispered. 'Worse. Look over there. It's Jesus and the guys.'

'So?' Tommo shrugged.

'So, we're not supposed to be here,' Pip reminded him. 'He specifically asked for just the three of them to go with him.'

'Well, we can't hear anything from over here. So if it's some kind of secret, we're fine.'

'But we can see. And if you can see what I can see, then I think maybe we're not supposed to be . . . seeing it!'

Strange as it may seem, Jesus was . . .

'Glowing,' said Pip. 'I think that's the word I would use for it.'

'I concur,' Tommo nodded. 'He is definitely . . . glowing. Though how or why I do not know.'

'Perhaps it would be best if we hid ourselves behind that small tree over there,' Pip suggested.

'Again, I concur,' Tommo said. 'But what about Bart?'

'Well, he's looking the other way,' Pip answered. 'And he's so busy trying to find that butterfly that I don't think he's actually noticed.'

'Thanks for the light, guys!' Bart called back, his head still buried in the bushes. 'I can see loads better.'

'Correction,' Pip said, 'perhaps he's noticed just a bit.'

Meanwhile, Jesus glowed brighter and brighter. And when he was so bright that Pip and Tommo could hardly stand to look at him, he was joined by two other shining figures.

Hands in front of their faces, eyes squinting just to see, Tommo and Pip tried to figure out who they were.

'Angels?' Pip wondered out loud.

'Could be,' Tommo nodded, 'but the one on the far side looks like he's carrying something.'

'Stone tablets!' Pip cried. 'The Ten Commandments! It's Moses!'

'But he died thousands of years ago!' gasped Tommo.

'After he led our people out of slavery,' Pip nodded. 'Amazing! And you know what? I think I've figured out who the other fella is, as well. Do you see the fiery chariot behind him?'

'Of course,' said Tommo. 'It's the prophet Elijah! Maybe the greatest prophet our people ever had.'

'So if these guys lived all those years ago,' Pip asked, 'what do you suppose they're doing here, with Jesus, now?'

'Dunno,' Tommo shrugged. 'Maybe God is trying to show us – well, that lot, strictly speaking – that Jesus is special like Moses and Elijah. And speaking of that lot – what's Peter doing?'

'He's waving his arms about. It looks like he's making the shape of a tent with his hands. Wish he'd speak up.'

'Flippin' fisherman,' Tommo grunted, straining to hear. 'Wait. You're right. He wants to build tents. One for each of them. So he can stay here and talk with them, I guess.'

'Fair enough,' said Pip. 'Those are three amazing individuals!'

Just then a cloud came down from the sky and surrounded them all. And a voice came out from the cloud. A voice so loud that no one could fail to hear it.

'This is my son,' the voice said. 'Listen to him!'

And when the cloud lifted, Moses and Elijah were gone, and Jesus was standing there, all alone.

'Guess one is more special than the rest, though,' Tommo concluded.

'Looks that way,' Pip agreed. 'So was that a vision – or did it really happen?'

'Don't know,' said Tommo, 'but we'd better get out of here. And we'd better find Bart.'

And so they did. And when they did, he was holding a butterfly in his hand.

'Dead Man's Bottom on my thumb!' he grinned. 'And just look at the expression on your faces. I knew you'd be amazed!'

'You think that's amazing,' grunted Tommo.

'You should have seen what we saw . . . ' added Pip.

But before they could say another word Bart had already bounded happily down the mountainside.

When they all reached the bottom, Jesus was there waiting.

'So where have you three been?' he asked.

'Ummm, up the mountainside, Jesus,' Pip muttered.

'That's right,' nodded Tommo.

Jesus looked a little concerned. A little worried. And maybe just a little annoyed.

'But I specifically asked just Peter and James and John to go with me.' And then he added, 'You didn't see anything, did you?'

And before Pip or Tommo could explain, Bart shouted, 'We did, Jesus! And it was amazing!'

'I see,' Jesus nodded, looking more anxious still. 'And what exactly did you see?'

'You'll never believe it, Jesus,' Bart beamed.

'Try me,' said Jesus.

'It's spectacular!' Bart added.

'I'll be the judge of that,' Jesus said.

'It's the most unbelievable thing ever!' Bart exclaimed.

'So tell me,' said Jesus. 'What was it?'

And Bart held out his thumb and said . . .

'A Dead Man's Bottom!'

There was a long and uncomfortable pause. And then finally Tommo muttered, 'It's a butterfly, Jesus.'

'Quite rare apparently,' mumbled Pip.

And Jesus grinned. Then he chuckled. Then he chortled. Then he laughed out loud and clapped his friends on the shoulders.

'You're absolutely right!' he agreed. 'That's an amazing butterfly, lads!'

And when he had walked away, still smiling, Pip and Tommo breathed a relieved sigh and Bart began to itch.

'What's up, big fella?' asked Pip.

'Lose your butterfly?' asked Tommo.

'No,' he said. 'It's that spider. The one that was living on my head in Bart Manor. He appears to have moved to the basement.'

And he shook his head. And his legs. And his Big Bart bottom.

About the Author

For a start, he's a storyteller. He goes to schools and churches and book festivals and tells Bible stores and folk tales and even some stuff he's made up himself. He's been doing this for something like twenty years and has been all over the world: North American and Europe and Africa and Asia and Australia and the Middle East. He loves to tell stories and he loves to travel, so if you know someone in Brazil who'd like a story, he'd love to go to South America, too.

He's also a writer. Bob has had more than fifty books published, most of them for

children. These include *The Lion Storyteller Bible, The Wolf Who Cried Boy, Bible Baddies* and *The Three Billy Goats' Stuff,* just to name a few.

And, finally, Bob is a minister. Or maybe that should be 'firstly' since that is what he was trained to do in the first place. Right now, he's working at Emmanuel Christian Church, in Pittsburgh (Go, Steelers!), Pennsylvania. His wife, Sue, is there too. And his son, Chris, who just married a girl called Mollie. And his daughter, Kari, lives in England with her husband, Martin, and their little boy Malachi.